The Journey To Be A Nurse

The Journey To Be A Nurse

Amanda Mehlhaff

Columbus, Ohio

The Journey To Be A Nurse

Published by Gatekeeper Press

2167 Stringtown Rd, Suite 109

Columbus, OH 43123-2989

www.GatekeeperPress.com

Copyright © 2021 by Amanda Mehlhaff

All rights reserved. Neither this book, nor any parts within it may be sold or reproduced in any form or by any electronic or mechanical means, including information storage and retrieval systems, without permission in writing from the author. The only exception is by a reviewer, who may quote short excerpts in a review.

ISBN (paperback): 97816629070500

Words of encouragement for a future nurse:

_____
_____
_____
_____
_____
_____
_____
_____
_____
_____
_____
_____
_____

"May he give you the desire of your heart and make all your plans succeed."

Psalm 20:4

You decided to go to college,
To be a future nurse.
With much expense for tuition,
Your debt went from bad to worse.

You arrived for your first day,
And didn't know one soul.
You looked around at strangers,
While the teacher took roll.

First semester was crazy,
You didn't know where to start.
But you realized you needed a planner,
And a large organizational chart.

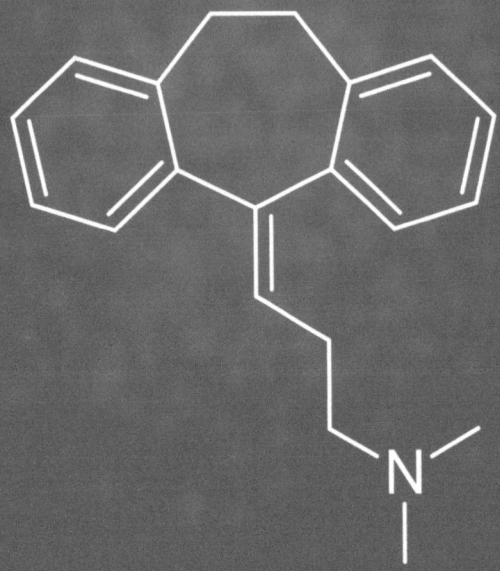

The following semester was busy,
And clinical was exciting.
But Pharmacology ruined the fun,
And all of the APA writing.

You may not have enjoyed some smells,
And were scared to stick a vein.
You didn't know how you'd make it through,
The amount of reading was insane.

At the start of every semester,
You knew it was going to be hard.
But you studied, studied and studied,
And got a good report card.

Needles no longer bothered you,
And you didn't mind the smell.
Many things came somewhat natural,
You were doing very well.

Though nursing school was stressful,
And you cried many tears.
You knew the things you were learning,
Were crucial for future years.

The last semester came fast,
You were ready to be done.
The end of nursing school was near,
As the months passed one-by-one.

Now it is time for graduation,
And you are kind of sad to go.
For the people that were strangers,
You came to closely know.

Friends became your family,
Helping each other through much stress.
But now you will all walk down the aisle,
In your graduation dress.

You will never forget your friends,
Or the important things you learned.
But know all of the hard work,
Is something that you earned.

Now you have your degree,
Take the NCLEX with no fear.
For you were meant to care for others,
Saving lives will be your career.

Nurses are truly special,
No other profession can compare.
Be proud of yourself, graduate.
You are almost there!

Never forget the smaller things,
Like a hug or a simple smile.
Graduate, go be wonderful,
And make your hard work worthwhile.

www.ingramcontent.com/pod-product-compliance
Lightning Source LLC
LaVergne TN
LVHW071733060526
838200LV00031B/482